AFRICAN FOLKTALES & ACTIVITIES

Retold by Louise Orlando

AFRICAN FOLKTALES & ACTIVITIES

Retold by Louise Orlando

SCHOLASTIC
PROFESSIONAL BOOKS

New York • Toronto • London • Auckland • Sydney

Cover design by Vincent Ceci
Cover illustration by Allan Eitzen
Interior design by Joy Jackson Childs
Interior illustrations by Michelle Hill
(Special thanks to Shannon Childs)

ISBN # 0-590-53542-0
Copyright © 1995 by Louise Orlando
All rights reserved.
Printed in the U.S.A.

12 11 10 9 8 7 6 5 4 3 2 1   1 2 3 4 5 6 / 9

UMUNTU NGUMUNTU NGOMNYE

Xhosa proverb, South Africa

People are people through other people

To Andrew

Here's to a wonderful adventure...

TABLE OF CONTENTS

INTRODUCTION

Imagine this: The sun has set in a fiery glow. It's pitch black. The only light for miles is the one from your campfire. Walk a few feet from it and you're enveloped in darkness. It's very still. Night birds call to each other. The fire snaps and crackles. In the distance you hear the low, powerful roar of a male lion. Closer to you, a voice as strong as the lion's, yet as captivating and steady as a stalking leopard, speaks. The voice belongs to the Storyteller. And in a magical way you are transported back to the beginning of time, when Earth was young and animals could speak. This is Africa.

For thousands of years, scenes like this have been repeated. Even today, in villages where electricity has yet to surge, storytelling, music, dancing, and singing continue to play an active role in community life.

Storytelling is an art that teaches a community's code of morality, relates a tribe's history, and explains natural wonders—all through entertainment. For example, children—and even adults—may discover and learn to appreciate the balance between humans and nature through tales about the evils of stealing, how the giraffe got his long neck, or the meaning of friendship. But most importantly, storytelling is a way of bringing people together and reminding them of their roots.

Many of the stories included in this book originated with the nomadic San (Bushmen) and the pastoral Khoi (Hottentots). Both the San and the Khoi, like the Native Americans of the United States and the Aborigines of Australia, were the original inhabitants of southern Africa, particularly South Africa. San cave paintings dating back over 40,000 years show that they lived in close harmony with nature. The San were known to take from the Earth only what they needed and were always respectful, saying thank you to the god who provided the food, and the animal who gave its life. Both the San's and the Khoi's closeness to nature also made them fine storytellers. How Humans Claimed Fire and Mr. Tread-Carefully are two examples of their fine stories.

Sadly, today there are few living San and Khoi. The group from which it is believed many southern African tribes originated, the Nguni, migrated southward from central Africa as European settlers were arriving in the southwest, at what is now called Western Cape. Both groups claimed land, set boundaries, and took from the San and Khoi their freedom. Many San and Khoi were taken as slaves and most were shot without reason. This was truly a sad period in the history of Africa. The San and Khoi who are alive today (their numbers are in the low hundreds) live primarily in the dry, desert regions of Namibia and Botswana.

There are hundreds and hundreds of tribes in Africa, speaking as many languages. Over the years, as tribe members intermarried, land borders opened, ideas, customs, and stories were shared.

As this is an excellent way to learn about how information spreads, it also poses a problem for any reteller of folk tales: how to attribute a story? It's important to keep in mind that any story in this book (and other folktale books) has likely been told by a number of different storytellers in their own special ways.

In keeping with the tradition of many African storytellers, these stories focus largely on animals. Animals were often given human attributes, such as the ability to speak, to judge right from wrong, and to make decisions as a way of teaching proper behavior. For these reasons, their names are always capitalized.

Also, by emphasizing animals, the stories may instill in children an appreciation for all creatures. Each mammal, bird, and lizard, right down to the tiniest insect, has an important role in our world's ecosystem. Whether or not your students ever encounter an elephant or rhino in person I hope they will gain an understanding, interest, and respect for our wildlife before it's too late. Extinction, after all, is forever.

These tales can also build on students' language arts, social studies, creative thinking, and art skills, while teaching them a respect for other cultures. Encouraging children to act out, think about, and add to stories will teach them to become storytellers, who in turn may one day pass on the stories of their own families and communities.

I spent nearly two years traveling throughout Africa. During my travels African women taught me how to prepare local dishes, like Senegalese fish and rice and Cameroon-style chili beans; I was challenged to a centuries-old game of *yote* by a chief's wife in Mali; and was laughed at by Zairian children as I attempted to carry a bucket of water on my head in typical African style. Every person I met and every place I visited opened my eyes and taught me a greater appreciation for cultures other than my own.

As you share these stories with your students, take time to set the scene, turn out the lights, and invite everyone to form a circle. And with your voice, just as storytellers for centuries have done, transport your listeners to the plains, forests, jungles, and rivers of Africa. Or play the accompanying audio tape, available from Scholastic Professional Books, which contains seven of these tales, professionally retold.

HOW TO USE THIS BOOK

Accompanying each story are facts about the African storytellers, the animals, or the story setting, in addition to activities. Mix and match ideas from different stories to suit your unit requirements and to enhance individual lessons while encouraging learning across the curriculum. Here are a few ideas you may want to try:

▶ Use a map of Africa to sharpen geography and thinking skills. Have a student identify the country a story comes from before reading the story. Ask students to describe the country through a map reading: is it mountainous, are there any major rivers, is the area a desert? How is the country similar to or different from the U.S.?

▶ Begin a math lesson with a story like *Giraffe's Long Neck*. Have children practice counting and addition skills while creating patterns with colored beads. Sit in a circle like the Masai, Samburu, and Zulu tribes of East and Southern Africa, and allow children to socialize as they work.

▶ Paint like a San. Using a variety of available ingredients, turn a science lesson into a hands-on experiment with students mixing and testing their own paints. Then put the paints to work on rocks, as the San do.

▶ Have students read stories aloud to build language and creative-thinking skills. First, ask them to read the stories to themselves, and think about areas needing special emphasis, a change of voice, or even sound effects to make the tale more interesting to the listener. (The accompanying audiotape, available through Scholastic Professional Books, contains a selection of stories from this book, with musical accompaniment and sound effects, and might serve as a model for students to emulate in their own storytelling efforts.) Encourage students to be creative and make their readings unique.

▶ Beginning a unit on weather, a discussion on elephants, or a lesson on honesty? Read *Elephant's Trick*, *When it Rains*, or *How Leopard Got His Spots*, paying particular attention to the focus of your unit. But most importantly, share these stories without losing the essence of sheer enjoyment and the fun of hearing a story read aloud.

WHEN IT RAINS

Many, many years ago, when the world was still quite young, and animals could speak, Thunder and Lightning lived on Earth in the form of Forest Buffaloes.

Lightning was young and very excitable. And like the Forest Buffalo, he had very poor eyesight and hearing. Lightning also had a short temper. Every time it rained he became enraged. The rain made it even harder for him to see and hear. It made him so angry, he knocked down and

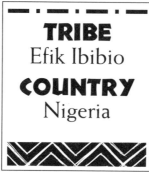

TRIBE
Efik Ibibio
COUNTRY
Nigeria

burned trees. Thunder, his mother, disliked her son's behavior. She could be heard trying to control him with her low booming voice, voice that shook the village trees.

The more Lightning burned, the more Thunder shouted. Trees and homes were destroyed faster than they could grow or be rebuilt. The destruction and the noise were unbearable! The other animals in the kingdom feared for their lives. Something had to be done with these disruptive neighbors.

So the animals held a secret meeting and called to their King. He was a good King and would certainly help them. He listened carefully for some time to the animals' complaints. Thunder and Lightning were indeed doing too much damage on Earth. After much thought, their King decided the only thing he could do would be to move mother and son to Sky. Here they could carry on without causing so much damage on Earth.

To this day, temperamental Lightning still knocks down and burns things and his mother can still be heard yelling at him. But they are far, far away and unless Lightning is very, very upset, animals and people on Earth are safe.

THE FACT IS...

Many of the Efik Ibibio tribe members live near the Niger River and make their living by fishing and trading.

The pirogue (as it's called in West and Central Africa) is one of the most common river boats in Africa. It's just like the dugout canoes made by Native Americans. Each boat is carved from one large tree trunk so there are no seams and thus, no leaks.

In areas of northern Nigeria, and in many parts of Africa, water is scarce. It's not unusual to see women walking miles with large buckets balanced on their heads carrying water from a well, spring, or other source.

Water is precious in these communities. The source is kept very clean and treated with extreme respect. For instance, it is forbidden to wash your body or belongings near a well.

TRY THIS:

FOCUS ON FACTS (Geography)

 Talk with the class about the country in which the story originated. (This is indicated at the beginning of the story.) Ask students to locate the country on a map of Africa. By studying the map's legend and the map itself, have students discuss features of the country's geography. For example, is the land mountainous? If so, in what areas? Are there major rivers? What are their names? What else do students notice? How is the country the same as or different from the one in which they live?

PATTERNING (Math)

Some stories lend themselves to math activities, especially lessons on patterns. You may want children to create necklaces like those the characters may have worn. Using different colored beads, children can create patterns such as 1, 2, 1, 2, 1, 2 or 1, 2, 3, 1, 2, 3, 1 2 3. Youngsters can also count the number of beads they used.

READ ALOUD, DISCUSS THEME (Language Arts)

Invite youngsters to talk about the theme or message of the story. Ask them to bring to class other books or stories that contain that theme. How are the stories the same? different?

CONSERVING WATER (Social Studies)

 As a group, make a list of the many different ways people use water, such as for washing, cooking, laundering, drinking, and so forth.

Then talk about what would happen if their community ran out of water. Jot these effects on the board and diagram how this loss would affect many aspects of the community. (For example, if there were no tap water for drinking, people would try to buy more bottled water, soda, and juice in cartons. More shoppers would go to the grocery stores more often. As a result, more delivery trucks would arrive in the community, causing . . .)

Talk with the group about what people can do—as a group and as individuals—to conserve this precious resource.

MAKE UP ORIGINAL STORIES (Language Arts)

 Invite youngsters to create their own stories to explain the origin of thunder or lightning. Children can dictate, draw, or write their work.

Students may want to suggest that animals, such as the elephant, the lion, or the gemsbok, cause thunder and lightning. If so, talk with them about some characteristics of these animals. That information can be woven into children's stories. For example:

▶ elephant: footsteps are heavy; trunk makes ear-splitting trumpet sound

▶ lion: has a low, steady, powerful roar; moves fast; has razor-sharp claws

▶ gemsbok: hooves are strong and pounding; horns make loud, cracking noise when males confront eachother

PRACTICE MAP SKILLS (Social Studies)

Using a map, mark Nigeria, where the Efik Ibibio originate. As a group, locate the Niger River. Trace its path through Niger and Mali. How might this river help the Efik Ibibio traders?

HOW LEOPARD GOT HIS SPOTS

The animals were sad; their good friend Ant had died. As was their custom, they sang as they prepared for his funeral. The sound of their singing voices floated high above the trees. Their music was more beautiful than any their kingdom had ever heard. As their voices lifted, so did their spirits on this special day when they bid their good friend Ant farewell.

As was the tradition in their society, family and friends of the dead gather to make the long walk to the sacred burial place. Today, Ant's family was joined in procession by Lion, Rhino, Elephant, Mongoose, Leopard, Tortoise, Monkey, and many, many others. And as was also the tradition, they sang as they walked.

TRIBE
Ashanti
COUNTRY
Ghana

Each animal contributed to the harmony and melody in his and her own way. Elephant used her trunk as a trumpet. Monkey, who was a talented drummer, kept the beat on a small drum made from a dried gourd. Lion used his powerful roar as a low, steady bass. Even Bongo, who is usually quiet, added a peaceful rhythmic

bleating. So, in spite of the sadness that brought them together, the friends were feeling quite happy. All, that is, except for the lovely golden —spotless—Leopard.

Leopard was hungry. He hadn't eaten in nearly two days and the pain and rumbling in his belly were growing stronger. He couldn't concentrate on the music. He walked slower and slower. He stopped singing. Leopard was about ready to leave and go in search of food when—as luck would have it—the procession passed an egg

farm. His face lit up.

'Mm, eggs,' he thought, as he licked his lips. 'A few eggs would make me feel better. I'll just sneak onto that farm for a quick bite, and jump back on the end of the procession. No one will notice.' Looking over each shoulder, Leopard crept away.

It was his lucky day indeed! The farm was empty, and lying out, as if expecting him, were baskets and baskets of fresh eggs. 'I'll just eat a few,' he thought.

Well, one egg turned into two, two turned into four, and four turned into a dozen. Soon all the eggs were gone. Leopard felt good. Without a word, he crept back into the proces-

sion. No one noticed his absence. He was so happy he started singing louder than all the others.

Meanwhile the Farmer returned. And to his great horror saw the broken shell remains of his eggs. He was furious. Who could have done such a horrible thing? Hearing the singing voices move down the road, the Farmer knew it had to be one of the animals. Off he ran, hollering for them to stop.

"Stop! Stop thief!" shouted the Farmer, nearly out of breath. "Which of you has eaten my eggs? I will punish the thief!"

Ant's eldest son stepped forward and said, "Farmer, the elder of our family recently died. The animals are walking with my family to the burial. I am sure none of them has eaten your eggs. There must be another who hides close by."

Farmer refused to believe this and would not let the procession continue. "You can prove your innocence by passing a little test," he declared. "I will build a fire and each of you will take turns jumping over it. The guilty ones will fall in."

Farmer built a roaring fire. One by one the animals took turns jumping over it. Finally, it was Leopard's turn. The others looked on impatiently.

"Hurry up," Elephant yelled. "Jump! We must move on."

And so Leopard jumped. His pure, golden body made a graceful arc as it glided through the air. Suddenly, an unseen force pulled him straight down into the fire. A sad silence fell over the group.

Leopard leaped out of the flames in pain. His beautiful fur coat was scorched black. The others were ashamed. Apologies were made to the Farmer, and the procession moved on in a gloomy silence—without Leopard. He was left on his own to nurse his wounds and the blackened scars—spots—that he now carries as a reminder of his greed.

THE FACT IS...

Ashanti stories are often told to pass on a moral message. Any story that has a moral is called an Ananse story (after Ananse, a "wise and clever" spider).

Drums play an important role in many African cultures. Like other African tribes, the Ashanti use talking drums to communicate with one another. Skilled drummers send various kinds of messages, warnings, and can even tell the history of a tribe by hitting different sized drums with either their bare hands, sticks, or a combination of the two.

The largest drums, which produce smooth, round, sounds at low pitches, are called female drums. "Male drums" make stronger, bolder sounds, at higher pitches.

Leopards are excellent climbers. They often spend their days sleeping in trees overlooking rivers. They begin hunting in the early evening, dragging whatever they kill up a tree out of reach of other predators.

Camouflage is important to animal survival. Leopard and zebra may look like they would be noticeable in the African bush but the opposite is true. A leopard's spots help him blend in with tree leaves, making him nearly invisible to passers-by.

If a zebra senses a nearby predator, he makes a warning snort to alert the others in his herd. Quickly, they move together. A predator with monochrome vision (one that can only see two colors, like a lion) is then left with the image of one huge striped animal, and may give up the hunt.

TRY THIS:

MORE ABOUT DRUMS (Language Arts)

Which of these names for common African drums do children recognize? Dondo, Timpani, Agdadza, Apinttintoa. Ask students to look through musical instrument catalogs for pictures or other information about these and other drums. You may also want to invite a musician to class to demonstrate different techniques for making drums "talk."

On another day, ask students to make a percussion corps. Have them tap or strike drums, table tops, or other materials to make interesting sounds and stories, or to "talk" like the drums of Africa.

DISCUSS THE MORAL (Language Arts)

Talk with the group about the moral, or lesson, of the story. Do students think Leopard "got" what he deserved? What makes them say that?

PLAY MATH GAMES (Math)

During a math lesson, ask students to give answers to simple addition, subtraction, multiplication, or division examples by tapping them out. How much are two 2s? Tap, tap, tap, tap.

THINK ABOUT CAMOUFLAGE (Science)

Discuss with the class how camouflage—the ability to disguise or conceal oneself—helps animals avoid being prey for enemies. On the board, list animals that use camouflage, such as some birds, some rabbits, some frogs, and some toads, among others.

Have students draw a picture that demonstrates how one of these animals disguises itself. Ask them to use crayons to draw a nature scene, such as the woods or a snowy field, on a large piece of drawing paper. Then have them create an animal from another piece of paper. Ask children to paste the animal in the scene so that it blends in with the background color(s). When classmates trade papers, see how quickly youngsters can locate the camouflaged animal.

THE EARTH KING'S FEAST

In a time before time, Earth was nothing more than a beautiful garden of plants and trees and rivers flowing with cool, clear water, none of which was eaten or drunk by any living creature. For you see, unlike today, all the mammals, birds, reptiles, fish, and insects lived peacefully in the Sky.

It was during this time, when Earth was a bountiful garden of delights, that Earth King invited the

TRIBE
Ekoi
COUNTRY
Nigeria/
Cameroon

glorious Sky Queen and her subjects to a special feast. The creatures could barely contain their excitement—for they had heard of the delights that awaited them on Earth.

Days before the feast Earth King made sure his trees were heavy with fruit, his grasses sweet and green, and rivers and streams running clear and cool. Earth was indeed a spectacular place and its King was proud and excited to be sharing it

with others.

When the day of the great feast arrived, Sky Queen and her subjects appeared before Earth King.

"My! My! My!" exclaimed the animals, their eyes wide in disbelief at what lay before them. Earth King smiled and invited them to take a  look around before the feast began. The animals thanked him and wandered off. Elephant found an enormous orange tree bursting with fruit. Carefully, he picked an orange and popped it in his mouth. It was clearly the most delicious food he'd ever tasted. He popped another and another into his wide mouth, his stomach rumbling happily. Monkey swung and jumped from tree to tree sampling oranges, mangos, guavas, and papayas.

Before long, all the animals had moved far, far away from the place where the feast was to be held. Earth King and Sky Queen were on their own. The rulers waited and waited for the animals to return. Sun made its way across the sky, still no animals returned. As Sun set, Sky Queen called out to her subjects, but they were scattered so far and wide that not a single one heard her calls.

Sky Queen felt sad. She knew that what lay here on Earth was much grander than what the animals had in her kingdom. So, as Moon rose full, Sky Queen returned to her land, alone. The animals, who eventually forgot the way back to their kingdom, remained on Earth, enjoying its riches, as guests of its generous King.

THE FACT IS...

Like many African tribes, the Ekoi are spread out across hundreds of miles of land. Their homes can be found in Nigeria and neighboring Cameroon.

Cameroon is a large country that supports a variety of ecosystems, ranging from dense tropical rainforest to semi-arid desert covered in scrub and thorn. Because there are so many different ecosystems, there are a number of animal species that are found nowhere else in the world but here. For example, the Mountain Gorilla is one such animal. Unfortunately, poachers (people who kill animals illegally) and hunters (who stalked them long ago) have killed so many gorillas that they are close to extinction.

TRY THIS:

ANIMAL SEARCH (Science)

 Invite students to select one animal, such as the monkey or elephant, and research the countries or regions on Earth in which that animal lives. After consulting encyclopedias or science books, ask students to present their findings to the class. They may want to draw maps and write text to support their work.

RETELL THE STORY (Language Arts)

Invite youngsters to retell the story through picture cards. As a group, list on the chalkboard the six main events of the story. Ask students to draw each scene on one of six blank cards, and to number the cards on the reverse sides. Have students pair off and retell the story to their partners using the cards as visual aids.

HOLD A FRUIT FESTIVAL (Social Studies)

Ask students to bring to class a variety of fruits, from apples and pears to papayas and bananas. Cut the fruits into bite-size pieces and set them out for small groups. Have them talk about the colors, the smells, and the textures. Then let children sample each one, eliciting descriptions of the fruits (bitter, sweet, tart, juicy).

ANIMAL FACTS (Science)

Students may enjoy making trading cards of pictures and information about animals mentioned in the story. Ask them to select one animal and find out what it eats, how long it lives, its habits, its enemies, and other information. Ask children to draw a picture on one side of a card and write interesting information on the back. Combine the cards in a pack and let students flip through it during free moments.

ELEPHANT'S TRICK

At one time, Warthog had two, beautiful ivory tusks that were longer than the tusks of any other animal, including Elephant. Naturally, Elephant was very jealous. He believed that, since he was so huge, he should have the grandest tusks, not a lowly Warthog. So it was out of jealousy that Elephant decided to play a cruel trick on Warthog.

Not aware of Elephant's feelings, Warthog accepted an invitation from the great beast to join him for breakfast.

On his way to Elephant's, Warthog passed his good friend Aardvark, who was just stepping out of his burrow. "Hello!" called Warthog. "I'm off to eat breakfast with Elephant. Imagine, that magnificent animal inviting me to share a meal!"

"Why, good morning, dear friend. An invitation from Elephant is unusual. Yes, I would be excited, too, but a word of warning: be careful," whispered his long-snouted friend. "Elephant is very clever and is not to be trusted. Be on guard during your visit for any tricks." Aardvark knew Elephant was

TRIBE
Nyanja
COUNTRY
Malawi

extremely jealous of Warthog's fine tusks and he hoped his small friend wasn't in danger.

"Thank you. I will remember your words. Good-bye!" And off Warthog trotted, his tail pointing toward Sun.

When Warthog arrived, Elephant was busy eating leaves from the fat Baobab tree. "Good morning, Warthog! Please, help yourself to those sweet roots," said Elephant kindly. "My, your tusks look lovely in the morning sun. You are so lucky to have such a magnificent pair."

"Oh, Elephant, you are too kind. I am quite proud of my long tusks, but you also have a handsome curly pair," smiled Warthog, happy to receive such a compliment from one like Elephant. "Please tell me, Large One, why is it that you invited me this morning?"

Elephant stopped eating and looked down at humble Warthog. He had a strange grin on his big face. "Kind Warthog, I have invited you here to ask a favor. I was wondering if you would mind lending me your great tusks. I've always wondered how I would look in ones

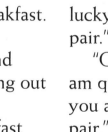

as large and beautiful as yours."

Warthog, overcome by Elephant's admiration and praise, forgot Aardvark's warning. "Of course you may try them on." Carefully, Warthog removed his long tusks and handed them to Elephant, whose small ones were tossed carelessly on the ground.

In two quick motions, Elephant had his guest's tusks on and ran to the River. Excited by his friend's happiness, Warthog followed, carrying Elephant's small tusks. Elephant stared and stared at his reflection. 'My, how grand I look with these long tusks,' he thought. 'These were definitely made for me, the largest animal on land. I must have them.'

"They look very nice on you," said Warthog honestly. He gave his friend some time to admire himself before asking for his precious tusks back. "Well, Elephant, it looks like rain. I must get moving to find shelter. As you know, I can't dig a hole to hide in. You know, sometimes I really envy Aardvark's long claws.

Oh well, here, I brought your tusks, so you may return mine now."

"HA! You foolish animal! You are no match for me!" trumpeted Elephant. "These tusks are mine. All mine! You can keep my small ones." And with that, Elephant thundered off crashing through the bush, knocking over trees.

Poor, poor trusting Warthog was in shock. His lovely tusks gone forever. Why hadn't he heeded Aardvark's advice? Now it was too late. To make matters worse, it started to rain. Sadly, Warthog walked back to his territory and again passed his friend's burrow.

On seeing Warthog's face, and the short tusks, Aardvark knew at once what happened. "Warthog!" called Aardvark. "Come, my dear friend. I know what evil Elephant did. From now on, he will pay for his wickedness, I promise you!"

"Please, don't try to make me feel better," moped Warthog. "There is nothing that can be done now. Elephant has run off, he will never return my tusks. I am stuck forever with these small ones."

Aardvark shook his long snout and in a deep voice said, "From now on, until the end of time, Elephant will pay for his theft. He will be hunted for those ivory tusks. He will never be safe. Whereas you, dear one, will live safely in a burrow from now on."

"That's very well for you to say, but I can't dig!" cried Warthog.

"Hush! You will live in my old burrows. You know that I have many and am always digging others. You will be safe for ever more!"

And from that day on, Warthog has lived safely in Aardvark's burrows and Elephant has been forced to run for his life from hunters after the stolen tusks.

Special Note: Some interpretations of this tale might make it seem that poaching is a punishment that elephants deserve. You might want to emphasize that this is not really the case— that killing elephants for their ivory is illegal and cruel, and not the fault of the elephants.

THE FACT IS...

 Much of Malawi's wildlife has been killed off by hunters and poachers. It wasn't until recently that laws were changed to protect the animals and the land they live on.

Lake Malawi is one of the world's largest lakes. It is also one of the few freshwater lakes that is home to dozens of varieties of colorful, tropical fish. But the lake may be heading for trouble if the Malawians don't protect this great resource from pollution and overfishing.

Right now, it's common to see fisherman bringing in baskets and baskets of undersized fish. Meanwhile, people use the lake for bathing, drinking, and dumping their wastes. Soon a lake that seemed like a sea will be nothing more than a polluted mess.

Malawians are known for their interesting carvings. Ebony, zebra wood (wood whose outer layers are white and inner layers black—it's a relative of ebony), and different types of soft stone like soap stone, are used to carve chairs, ritual masks, tables, animal statues, and games. Experienced carvers can turn one piece of wood into a table—without cutting it into pieces or using any nails.

Before carvers begin work, they look at their material and make a plan. For instance, before carving a mask, they plan where the eyes, nose, mouth, and any special symbols must go. It's not unusual to see people sketching their design on paper or in the sand before beginning work. It is also true that experienced carvers can pick up a chunk of wood and carve a perfect piece without ever putting pencil to paper.

A full-grown elephant can use his trunk to suck up nearly 14 liters of water at one time.

Healthy adult elephants may eat nearly 150 pounds of food a day.

 Aardvarks are nocturnal animals. At night they roam the bush looking for tasty meals of ants and termites. They use their long sharp nails to dig out insect mounds. Once in the nest, they use their long sticky tongues to catch and eat the squiggling masses.

Warthogs are herbivores. They eat short grasses and sometimes fruits, roots, bulbs, and tubers. They often drop down on their hairy front knees to eat.

Warthog gets its name from the large warts on its face. Males have four warts, females have two.

Aardvarks and warthogs have very poor eyesight. But their sense of smell and hearing are topnotch—it's likely they'll "see" you before you see them.

TRY THIS:

ANIMAL DRAMA (Language Arts)

Have children form small groups. Assign an animal role to each child and let him or her act out Elephant's Trick. Encourage them to create dialogue for additional animals, in keeping with the story's plot.

WRITE A NEW TALE (Language Arts)

What would happen if aardvarks filled in their old burrows? Where would animals like the warthog, hyena, and porcupine live?

MAP SEARCH (Geography)

Malawi is a small country in Central Africa. Bordered on the west by Mozambique and on the east by Tanzania and Zambia. Stick the Map It! card here. Locate Lake Malawi on the map. Next, looking at the entire African continent, ask which other large lakes students can identify.

FISHY FACT-FINDING (Geography)

Encourage older children to visit the library and find out more about the freshwater tropical fish that live in Lake Malawi.

MR. TREAD-CAREFULLY

For as long as anyone can remember, Chameleon has had the nickname of Mr. Tread-Carefully for he is one of the wisest, most cautious animals in the world. His every thought and movement is so calculated that it often takes Chameleon ages to do anything—even walk to the end of a branch. For this reason, Mr. Tread-Carefully was chosen to deliver a very important message to the Humans living on Earth.

TRIBE
Khoi
(formerly known
as Hottentots)
COUNTRY
Namibia/
Southern Africa

The message was: Humans will never die. When their jobs on Earth are complete, they will go away, but will return, like the moon, at different times.

Chameleon understood the importance of the message, and was honored to be trusted with its delivery. In his mindful and conscientious way, he memorized the message. And not until he was absolutely certain that he memorized it correctly did he begin the long journey to the place where Humans lived.

This was his first trip across Earth, so he was particularly cautious. Days and nights and days and nights passed. Small Chameleon repeated the message over and over to himself as he crossed deserts, climbed mountains, and walked through jungles.

Many moons had come and gone, and not a word was heard from the reptile. The Creator wondered if something went wrong. This was such an important message he decided it would be best to send a second messenger. The swift Hare was chosen.

The message was repeated: Men and Women will never die. When their jobs on Earth are complete, they will go away, but will return, like the moon, at different times.

Hare repeated the message quickly and was off.

He covered the same ground Chameleon had but in a fraction of the time. Soon Hare passed Chameleon but didn't see him because he was moving so quickly. Hare reached the Humans long before Mr. Tread-Carefully.

He stood before the Humans and began to speak. Oh no! What was it he was meant to say? He forgot the message! The Humans stared at him. He concentrated. He scratched his head. He sat down. He stood up. He jumped up and down. Hare thought and thought, trying hard to remember the exact words. The Humans waited patiently.

"Hmm," said Hare as he scratched his head for the fourth time, "The message is, the message is. . .Oh yes, the message is this: When Humans finish their jobs on Earth, they will die. Never, ever to return again." With that, Hare bounded off into the bush for a better look around this strange place.

By the time Chameleon arrived it was too late. The wrong words were spoken, so this earthly tribe must live—and die—by these words forever.

THE FACT IS...

Khoikhoi (as the Khoi are also known) means "men of men" in their language.

The name Hottentot came from the European pronunciation of a sound they heard the Khoi repeating aloud as they danced: *hautitou*.

The Khoi are believed to have migrated from Central Africa (possibly Malawi) sometime between the 13th and 14th centuries. They arrived after the San.

The Khoi were pastoralists. They moved their cattle and themselves as seasons changed and finding new grazing land became necessary. Some historians believe that cattle diseases, which wiped out whole herds, and the arrival of the Bantu (which means Blacks) and Europeans in southern Africa pushed the Khoi off the land, forcing them to turn to the sea for survival.

 The African flap-necked chameleon can grow to nearly a foot in length from the tip of its nose to the tip of its tail. It's common to see these slow-moving reptiles sitting very, very still in trees as they wait for insects to come by.

Namibia is a land of many natural wonders, including Sossusvlei, the largest sand dunes in the world (over 1000 feet high), and Fish River Canyon, second in size only to the Grand Canyon.

An old San story claims that a group of strangers strayed across an area of private property and were found by the land's hunters. The hunters, enraged at the intrusion of these strangers, killed everyone but the women. One new mother was so distraught at the death of her child that she cried and cried. She cried so much her tears formed a huge lake. A few days under the hot desert sun dried the lake up completely, leaving only a large salt pan—Lake of a Mother's Tears or Etosha Pan, as we call it today.

TRY THIS:

CHAMELEON QUALITIES (Language Arts)

 Some say calling a person a chameleon is a compliment, others say it isn't. Have a class debate. Ask: Is it a good quality to be able to change and behave differently depending on the crowd you're with? Or is it better to remain as you are, and be true to yourself?

WHO'S TO BLAME? (Language Arts)

Sometimes acting slowly can cause problems (think about doctors in an emergency room). In this story, is chameleon partially responsible for the eventual death of Humans? Or is it all the careless hare's fault for not taking the time to memorize the message?

COMPARING TALES (Language Arts)

Tell the Aesop's story of the Tortoise and the Hare. Talk about how "slow and steady" won that race. Compare the two stories.

SPECIES SORTING (Science)

There are quite a few species of reptiles, amphibians, and fish that can change color to match their surroundings or to attract a mate. Visit the library to find out more about these animals. Are any indigenous to your area?

THE PLAINS OF AFRICA (Geography)

Namib is a Khoi word for plain. Study the map. Have students point out major areas of Namibia, such as Sossusvlei, Fish River Canyon, and Etosha Pan.

A JOURNEY OF LIFE AND DEATH

Long, long ago, in the beginning of time, when Earth and its inhabitants were very young, there was no Death as we know it today. Death was kept under the watchful eye of the Creator and not allowed to roam Earth freely. At times this was most trying for the Creator since Death was forever begging and pleading to be set free.

One day, tired of all the noise Death was making, the Creator gave in. Death was granted permission to move freely about Earth. But at the same time, a promise was made to people: Humans would not die.

This was terrific news, because the thought of leaving their family and such a beautiful place as Earth saddened Man and Woman. But still, they couldn't help but wonder how to protect their family with Death moving freely.

TRIBE
Mende
COUNTRY
Sierra Leone

The Creator explained that a basket of skins would be delivered to Humans. As Man, Woman and the members of their large tribe aged, they would simply take off their old skins and put on new ones. Thus, they did not surrender their lives to Death.

Now, this basket of an infinite number of skins was entrusted to Jackal, a wily creature who the Creator was certain would deliver the skins safely and quickly to Humans.

Jackal wasn't gone long when his stomach began grumbling and rumbling with hunger. He was so hungry he could think of nothing else but food. He had to eat now.

Lifting his head, he sniffed deeply. Turning his pointy nose, he sniffed again. A huge grin spread across his face. He smelled food and it wasn't far off. He would stop for a quick meal before continuing his journey.

The delicious smells led Jackal deep into the forest to a huge party. When the guests saw Jackal, he was immediately welcomed and handed a bowl of steaming potato stew. When he finished that, he ate some nuts, then a few eggs, and finally some juicy mangos. As he ate, he bragged to the others about his job. They were very impressed, and each animal wished he or she were the one entrusted with such a mission.

By the time the meal was finished, Jackal's belly was so full and round he could barely walk. 'I'll take a quick nap under that tree,' he thought. 'When I wake, I'll run twice as fast to Humans. No one will ever know.' He was fast, fast asleep before his small head touched the ground, his whiskers twitching peacefully.

One hour passed, two hours passed, three hours passed. Jackal barely stirred. Sun had set and the forest was pleasantly warm—just the right temperature for sleeping and just the right temperature for 15-foot Python to start moving. As Jackal slept (snoring quietly), Python slithered closer and closer to him. (Now, it should be told that Python is a very sly creature, trusted by no one.) While Jackal was eating, Python (who was hiding nearby) heard him telling the others about the precious gift he was bringing to Man and Woman. Python could think of nothing better—he wanted those skins.

Silently, Python moved his long, muscular body closer and closer to Jackal. Slipping his sleek head under the handle, Python pulled the basket into the deep, dark forest where he lived.

Jackal awoke the next morning with Sun beating down on his face. Slowly he stood up, stretched his stiff legs and wondered where he was. Suddenly he remembered.

Turning around and around, he looked frantically for the basket. It was gone. But Python's legless tracks were not. Jackal knew who had the basket and he knew Python would never return it. There was only one thing he could do and that was to break the news to Man and Woman.

They were outraged. Death was loose and now they had no defense against him. Humans called to the Creator, ordering him to tell Python to give back the skins. The Creator answered, "I have listened and acted on your demands for a long time. You want too much, much more than any other creature on Earth. This time you will suffer the consequences. You will die when you grow old."

As for Python, well, he still has the basket and changes his skin as it ages. Surprisingly, he shared the basket with other snakes. To this day, many humans (without really knowing why) dislike snakes. As for Jackal, well, he's still upset about his mistake and rarely shows his pointy face around us.

THE FACT IS...

 Pythons eat everything from monkeys to rodents to small crocodiles. They are the only snake large enough to eat a child (but rarely do).

Snakes are not slimy reptiles. Smooth scales, which are soft and dry, cover their strong muscular bodies.

Africa's largest snake is the African rock python. It is also a protected species.

Pythons eat by first wrapping their bodies around their prey and squeezing it until it suffocates. Then, like other snakes, they swallow the animal whole by unhinging their jaws.

Sierra Leone is a small West African Country. Like many other West African countries bordering on the Atlantic Ocean, fishing plays a large part in the community's daily life.

TRY THIS:

ANIMAL LOCOMOTION (Science)

In the story, Python moved with his long, muscular body, slithering forward. Jackal walked with his legs. Hold a discussion of the different ways in which animals move. As a group, create a chart that summarizes what children know. For example:

NAME OF ANIMAL	HOW IT MOVES
python	crawl
jackal	with 4 legs
bird	fly
fish	swim
kangaroo	with 2 legs

WHAT DOES RESPONSIBILITY MEAN? (Social Studies)

Jackal was entrusted with a special responsibility, but he was careless. Have children ever been given a special job? What was it? How did they do? How did they feel when the job was completed? What advice would they give to other children who also have special tasks to complete? Let children summarize by creating a booklet of advice to be shared with children from a younger class.

HOW ZEBRA GOT HIS STRIPES

Sun rose, as it did each morning over the vast African plains, bathing the land in a brilliant golden light. On this particularly clear, crisp morning, all was quiet, except for the steady munch, munch, munching of the animals.

Lion, tired after a night of hunting, rested quietly in the tall grasses. Rhino slowly chewed a mouthful of tender leaves, enjoying Sun's warmth on his leathery back. Small Duiker, skipped about stretching her legs after a night hiding in the deep bush. And of course, there was Zebra. Zebra did what Zebra always did: eat, eat, and eat some more. The others called him a glutton, but Zebra didn't care. He just kept eating and his belly just kept growing.

As Sun rose higher and higher in the cloudless blue sky, the animals became increasingly restless. Today was their big day. Today, they would choose their coats and horns. Up to now, the animals, although different shapes and sizes, all had plain, drab coats and no horns. Elephant didn't have a trunk and Lion didn't have a mane. Now the coats and horns were ready, and were left for the animals in a cave

> **TRIBE**
> Angoni
> **COUNTRY**
> Malawi

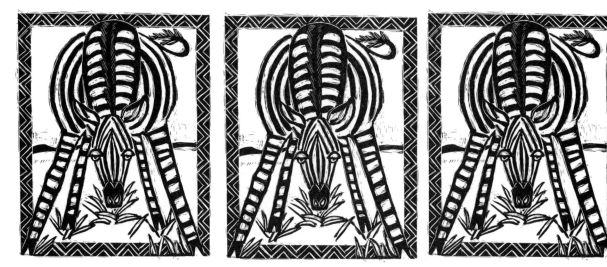

44

near the Great Lake. Raising his large head, Lion sniffed the air and decided it was time to go. He wanted to be first and choose the most magnificent coat available. He wasn't interested in horns, since he already had a very sharp set of teeth and claws. Off he ran. Elephant, seeing Lion go, decided to follow. He also thought very highly of himself and wanted to find something to distinguish himself from the others. By midzday, all the animals, except Zebra, were at the cave.

Meanwhile, Zebra just kept eating and eating, lifting his head only to look for more sweet grass.

One by one the animals returned. Lion, who was first in the cave, now had an elegant golden-brown coat and a very majestic mane of thick black hair. He was proud of his new look. He strutted back and forth with his head held high, roaring as loudly as he could. Elephant arrived next. His coat was nothing special, a simple dull gray with a skinny, bare tail. What was spectacular about his choice though, was his new trunk and long, ivory tusks. With his trunk alone, he could pull up trees, reach tender leaves from high branches, and spray water on his back. Yes,

Elephant had made a smart choice.

Duiker chose a lovely soft gray-blue coat, and two small, straight horns which he pointed towards his back. Even large Buffalo looked impressive. Her new black coat made her body look very big and grand. And oh, those horns! They were a huge, massive curved set that, when positioned just so, made her forehead look very broad and smart.

Lion strutted by Zebra and growled at him to hurry up, otherwise all the coats and horns would be taken. Zebra snorted, and with his mouth already full, took another bite.

When Sun began to set, Zebra decided he must visit the cave. On his way there he passed Rhino coming in the opposite direction. Poor nearsighted Rhino! His new coat was many sizes too big. And his horns! Rhino had selected two horns of different sizes; and to make matters worse, he put them on his nose! Shaking his head, Zebra moved on.

Zebra entered the cave. In the disappearing light Zebra could see that all the horns were gone. There was a coat left. It was an ugly, gaudy coat of black and white stripes. 'Oh well,' he thought. 'Maybe there is another coat tucked away in here somewhere, but I'm so hungry I don't feel like looking."

So he put the striped one on and, surprisingly, it fit quite well. Zebra didn't care what it looked like anyway. He just walked outside and began eating again. Slowly he made his way back to his favorite patch of grass near the other animals. It was dark by the time he returned, so no one noticed his new coat.

When Sun came up the next day, Elephant with his sharp eyes was the first to see Zebra. He started laughing. And then Eland with his handsome hind stripes, and Giraffe with her elegant, long neck and bold spots, began laughing, too. But Zebra didn't care. 'Let them laugh,' he thought. 'It doesn't matter what they think. I like my coat, it fits quite well. Besides, I'm hungry.'

So to this day, Zebra wears his striped coat with pride, and doesn't concern himself with what others think because he's too busy eating and eating and eating.

THE FACT IS...

Lake Malawi is one of the world's largest lakes. It's so big that it gives the appearance of being an ocean. Occasionally there are waves big enough to bodysurf on.

Like snowflakes and fingerprints, no two zebras are alike.

 The Quagga is an extinct species of zebra. It lived in Southern Africa and was hunted to extinction for it's half-striped, half-plain coat. The last Quagga died in 1883 in an Amsterdam zoo. The Cape Mountain Zebra is the only other endangered zebra.

It's hard to believe, but zebras' stripes are actually excellent camouflage, even on an open plain. When predators are near, zebra may be seen moving together in one large group—creating the illusion of one huge series of stripes. They end up confusing potential attackers by appearing to be one large animal.

Lions are zebras' biggest predators. But zebras never give in without a fight, and are capable of breaking a lion's jaw with a swift kick of their back legs.

TRY THIS:

MIXED-UP ANIMALS (Art)

There are giggles in store for the class as they create imaginary animals with unexpected features. Start by asking the class to name some distinguishing animal characteristics as mentioned in the story, such as tusks on the rhino, a trunk on the elephant, stripes on the zebra, and a thick, black mane on the lion. Using crayons and drawing paper, ask students to draw only the body of one of these animals. Then have them add a feature of a different animal. Children may create an elephant with stripes or a lion with a trunk. Have youngsters give names to their new creations and display the mixed-up animals on a bulletin board for all to enjoy.

HOW FAST CAN THEY GO? (Science)

Ask students to look in science books and encyclopedias to find out how fast the animals named in the story can move. Which can run faster, the elephant or the zebra? the rhino or the lion? Create a chart that lists the animals' speeds in order from fastest to slowest.

IF I WERE AN ANIMAL (Science)

Ask youngsters to imagine they are an animal from the story. Which animal would they like to be? Why? Do children admire one animal's appearance? speed? cleverness? Have youngsters write and draw why they would like to be that animal.

GIRAFFE'S LONG NECK

Long, long ago, in a part of Africa where the plains stretch for miles and miles, and trees were few and far between, a year-long drought plagued the land. Waterholes dried up, grass turned brittle and brown. The only green for miles was at the top of the thorny acacia trees. So high up were these sweet small leaves that the animals could only look at them longingly. It was these leaves that Giraffe and Rhino discussed.

"Look at those leaves, my friend," said Giraffe, whose short neck and powerful legs made her look no different than Waterbuck, Eland, and Kudu. "While they sit up there, we are hungry down here. Oh, how I wish I could reach up and take a bite."

"Hrmmph," said near-sighted Rhino who wasn't much of a talker. "If you want them so badly, speak to the Herbalist."

"Rhino! That's a brilliant idea. He will surely help," exclaimed Giraffe,

TRIBE
Unknown, possibly Masai
COUNTRY/ REGION
East Africa

her eyes sparkling.

So together, they headed towards the setting sun and the Herbalist's home. They stopped only once on their long walk to nibble some grass. They had such a long way to go.

By the time they reached the Herbalist's round mud hut it was morning. The Herbalist worked busily building a fire.

"Good morning, " called the two friends. A short man dressed in brightly colored fabrics looked up with a smile. "We have a problem."

And so Giraffe explained how the lack of rain was driving the animals in search of food. She talked about the acacia trees, and how she and Rhino wished they could eat the tender, green leaves, but neither could climb trees or reach high enough to take a bite.

The serious little man listened carefully, nodding his head and finally smiling. "Ah, my friends. You have come to me with a problem that I can solve. I know a magic herb that will cause your legs and necks to grow. You will be so tall that leaves on all the treetops will be yours. The problem is, I must go and collect this plant. Please, come back at sunrise tomorrow." And with that, the Herbalist disappeared inside his hut.

Giraffe and Rhino could hardly believe their ears. They planned to meet at the Herbalist's hut before sunrise so as not to be late. Giraffe walked off toward a waterhole, which was actually more mud than water. And Rhino wandered in search of food, for all the excitement made him very hungry.

The next day, as promised, Giraffe waited just before sunrise near the Herbalist's hut. She waited and waited, but Rhino didn't appear. When Sun rose, Rhino was still nowhere in sight. Giraffe walked slowly toward the Herbalist's hut. Once again he was busy building his morning fire. A small bundle of unusual looking green and orange leaves rested near a blackened pot.

"Good morning, friend. I am glad to see you, but where is Rhino?" asked the Herbalist as he untwisted one of the strange dried roots he wore on a leather cord around his neck.

"I don't know. When we left you yesterday, he said he was very hungry and went in search of food. I know he will come. Can we wait a bit longer?" Kind Giraffe didn't want her friend to miss out on the magic. After all, it was Rhino's idea to come here in the first place.

While they waited, the Herbalist finished building his fire and had started on his morning chores. Sun rose higher and higher in the sky. It grew very hot. By midday, there was still no sign of Rhino. The small man was hot and angry. "Listen, my friend, Rhino was told to be here at sunrise. He is still not here. I can wait no longer. Here is the magic herb." He put the mysterious-looking leaves in front of Giraffe. "You must eat them now before all the magic goes out. Your friend Rhino is too late."

With that, the Herbalist went into his cool hut, shut the door, and lay down to take a nap. Giraffe ate all of the special herbs. As she finished the last bite, she began to feel a little funny. A strange prickly, tingly, feeling crept over her.

Giraffe looked down at her legs. Could it be? Yes. Yes! They were growing!

Trying to remain calm, she closed her eyes and took a slow, deep breath. When she finally lifted her long lashes, she couldn't believe what she saw. Everything had changed! She no longer looked up at the lovely acacia trees. Now she looked over them! The magic herbs worked! Moving carefully, not yet sure about her new legs, she walked to the thorny tree. With eyes opened wide she stretched her long neck, opened her mouth and took a bite of the most delicious leaves she had ever tasted.

Now Rhino, who had found a patch of tasty grass and spent the night and most of the day eating it, suddenly remembered his promise to Giraffe. Running as fast as his short legs would carry him, he arrived at the Herbalist's hut near sundown. It was too late. Poor Rhino saw Giraffe with her long legs and graceful neck eating happily from the top of the acacia. Turning to the Herbalist, Rhino asked about his share of the magic plant. The Herbalist shook his head, and Rhino knew there wasn't any left.

Furious with himself, Rhino lost his temper and chased the Herbalist into the bush behind his hut. To this day Rhino is known for his particularly short temper and Giraffe is still the only animal (besides those who climb) who can eat comfortably from treetops.

THE FACT IS...

The Masai are well-known cattle herders and fierce warriors. They move their cattle between Kenya and Tanzania in search of grass.

The Masai wear colorful blankets draped over their shoulders and rows and rows of beads and copper jewelry on their arms, necks, and legs.

The Masai warrior's diet consists solely of cow's blood (it's believed for the salt and other nutrients) and milk.

 Young Masai warriors have long plaited hair, which they cover in a mixture of animal fat and the deep red local soil. They carry long spears (nearly six feet long) with a sharpened edge that itself is about three feet. Spears are used for hunting, or with shields made from animal skin for war.

In the Masai culture, the number of colorful beads a woman wears around her neck is one sign of her husband's wealth. The more beads, the wealthier he is. To many, the different colored beads have special meanings. For instance, green may represent wealth, red might mean passion or intense love.

Masai women take pride in stringing their beads. Each bead is selected with care. Often women will trade with one another for particular beads. Each woman creates a pattern that may tell a story.

Herbalists, witch doctors, and magicians all play important roles within many African tribes. It's not unusual for tribal members to consult such a person before moving into war, getting married, or going against a tradition. During a crisis the people will often look to this man or woman for advice.

Male giraffes may weigh over 2,500 pounds and stand about 18 feet high. Their legs are so powerful, they can kill a 400-pound lion with one kick.

Giraffes are about six feet tall at birth. They give birth standing up, which means the baby has about a five foot drop to the ground.

Humans and giraffes have only seven bones in their necks.

Many people believe giraffes are silent, but they actually make quiet grunting and moaning noises.

Some giraffes can run as fast as 30—35 mph.

TRY THIS:

PERSONAL CHARACTERISTICS (Social Studies)

Ask children to suggest words that describe each character. For example, children may describe Rhino as undependable and Giraffe as prompt. Then talk about which of these traits are important for the children to have. Why is it important to be prompt? What happened to Rhino as a result of his tardiness? What do children think is the overall message of the story?

BEADS TELL ABOUT US (Math)

Make available a variety of colored beads, painted dry pasta shapes, seeds, or other objects suitable for stringing. Let each student choose his or her own beads. Next, have them assign a meaning to the different beads before stringing. (For example, blue beads may indicate how many brothers they have.) Encourage students to share their stringed stories with the class.

DID YOU KNOW? (Science)

As a class, make a list of animals with distinguishing physical characteristics. For example: zebra—stripes, elephant—trunk, elk—antlers, beaver—flat tail, lion—main.

Next to each animal write as many interesting facts as the class knows about this characteristic. For example:

ANIMAL	CHARACTERISTIC	FUN FACTS
elk	antlers	shed them each year grow back bigger following year only on males act as protection when sparring with other males

LAZY, LAZY HARE

Each day Sun shone brighter and hotter. And each day the animals looked up at the sky for a sign of rain. The land slowly dried up. Grass turned brown. Small bushes, whose roots were weak and thin, rolled about. The animals needed water.

Late one day, as Sun dipped behind a distant mountain, the animals gathered to talk about the problem of water. Soon they would be forced to walk miles in search of it. A sad silence fell over the group. Then, a small, steady voice spoke up. Wise Tortoise had something to say.

"Why don't we dig a waterhole?"

TRIBE
Yoruba
COUNTRY
Nigeria

he suggested, in his slow, careful manner.

The others blinked, thinking about the suggestion.

Smiles crossed their faces. "What an excellent idea!" everyone shouted. So when Sun rose the next day, the animals searched together for the right spot to start digging. As luck would have it, Elephant found an underground spring that morning.

Everyone joined in the digging. Aardvark used his long claws. Rhino kicked soil and rocks away. Even Snake helped by wrapping her long, muscular body around stubborn

 roots to pull them out. Everyone worked. Everyone, that is, but Hare.

Lazy, lazy Hare watched the others work as he lay hidden behind a large rock, his feet propped up on a round, empty calabash. He couldn't believe it took so many animals so long to dig a hole! He was thirsty and really wished they would hurry. You see, Hare had a plan for getting the water.

Finally, the hole was complete. Hare watched from his hiding place as the animals took turns drinking the clear water. Hare's throat itched with anticipation. Tortoise, being the slowest, was last to drink. Just as Tortoise lifted his small head, Hare went into action. He yelled and banged on the calabash with a big stick.

Oh, what a racket he made! It was horrible and wicked, wicked Hare knew it. The noise frightened all the animals—including mighty Elephant—away. Alone now, Hare crept down to the waterhole. He took a long, slow drink of the cool, clear water. He drank so much his belly swelled and swelled until it was as round as a pumpkin. When he was no longer thirsty, he dove in  head first. He laughed as he washed and scrubbed the soles of his dirty feet and behind his pointy ears. With his thirst quenched and clean, Hare hopped away.

The next day the others returned to their waterhole and to their surprise the clear water was muddy!

With a mighty roar Lion pointed to the spoor leading straight into the well. "These are Hare's prints. He tricked us! He was too lazy to help us and now he drinks our water and worse, bathes in it! We must teach him a lesson."

The animals put their heads together. Again, wise Tortoise had a suggestion. He whispered it to his friends. "Hare will be sorry he was so lazy," smiled Tortoise.

To carry out Tortoise's plan, everyone gathered the stickiest tree sap they could find. The animals piled the chocolate-colored resin in front of the waterhole. Monkey, the most creative and the one with the lightest touch, carefully formed the sticky sap into the shape of a Human he had seen on one of his travels. The Human  was made to look as if she were washing near the well.

Later that day, as was expected, Hare returned to the well for a drink. The other animals hid nearby. There sat the Human. Hare called out a greeting to her. No response.

Hare took a step closer and repeated his greeting. Still, no response. He moved closer and tapped her on the shoulder. Hey! What was this? His paw was stuck. He pulled and pulled put couldn't free it. This wasn't a real Human after all! Hare panicked. Not thinking, he used his feet as leverage against the sticky Human. Now all four paws were stuck. "Oh, help!" he wailed in pain and fright. "This

Human has me and plans to eat me!"

At that moment, the others jumped out from their hiding places and glowered at Hare. "You thief!" they yelled. "You were too lazy to help us. Go away from here. You do not belong with us, you lazy animal!"

Hare was set free, and he ran and ran far away from there, never to be seen again!

THE FACT IS...

Like many other African stories, this one may have been told to teach children a lesson, such as the importance of cooperation and hard work.

 Through this tale, children also learn to respect their water sources, which in many areas of Africa are scarce. As a result, it's a rare sight to see people washing clothes or themselves in the same place they collect drinking water.

It's common to see Africans carrying everything from buckets of water, to huge bags of charcoal, or bunches of bananas on their heads. Many African women and men can carry objects weighing over 20 percent of their body weight on their heads. It's a great way to carry things, since it leaves hands free to bargain in the markets or hold onto small children.

The Yoruba live in southern Nigeria. Their kingdoms are thousands of years old. Their language is one of Africa's most widely spoken.

Spoor is another name for any trace of an animal. People studying or hunting an animal track it by its spoor to learn more about it. Good trackers can tell an animal's size, whether or not it was running, and when it passed a spot, just by the spoor.

Hares live on grasses that provide them with the water they need to live.

Hares and rabbits are different. Hares have long ears, short tails, and long legs built for speed and jumping.

Hares never dig burrows. Instead they make their homes in tall grass or near bushes where they can hide.

TRY THIS:

COMPARE TALES (Language Arts)

 Bring to class, or ask children to bring in, other folktales that contain a hare and a tortoise. After reading each story aloud, talk about the personal traits of the characters. (For example, in *Lazy, Lazy Hare*, Tortoise is slow, but wise. Hare is lazy.) In what ways is the tortoise and hare from each story alike? different?

RETELL THE TALE (Language Arts)

Children will enjoy retelling the story by writing and drawing about key events in an accordion book. Show how to make an accordion book by taping sheets of paper to each other on the short ends and folding the sheets backward and forward so that they open like accordion pleats.

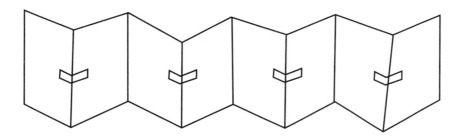

Have youngsters write the title on the cover, along with their name as story reteller. As a group, list 6 main story events on the board. Have children write an event on each page of their own book and draw a corresponding picture. Key events may include:

1. Animals gather to talk about the problem of a lack of water.
2. With Tortoise's suggestion, we dig a water hole.
3. From his hiding place, Hare yells and bangs on a calabash with a big stick.
4. Animals run from the water hole. Hare drinks and bathes by himself.
5. Animals discover Hare's trick. They make a Human shape from sap.
6. Hare returns and gets stuck to the sap. He is set free and never returns again.

HOW HUMANS CLAIMED FIRE

Long, long ago, in the beginning of time before Humans had control of Fire, Ostrich was considered one of the most loyal, yet stubborn, creatures on Earth. For this reason, she was chosen for a very special job.

Mantis, the Creator's chief assistant, chose Ostrich to guard Fire. Mantis believed that fire was so powerful it would destroy anyone who used it. He also believed that any creature—human or animal—who was smart enough to take Fire from Ostrich deserved to have it, and thus would use it wisely. So with that, Mantis delivered Fire to Ostrich with strict instructions to guard it with her life.

For years Ostrich hid Fire under one wing without anyone knowing about it. Until one hot, hot day when she took to walking about with her wings outstretched to cool off. As it hap-

TRIBE
San (formerly known as Bushmen)
COUNTRY
Botswana/ Southern Africa

pened, this was also the day a very clever, sharp-eyed San was out walking and spotted Fire under her wing. 'What a wonderful thing Fire must be,' he thought. 'I'm sure I could think of many ways to use it.' He wanted Fire more then ever.

San knew Ostrich was too stubborn to give Fire up for no reason. She was obviously hiding it for a purpose. So he thought and thought about how to get it from her. One morning the answer came to him.

With a sly smile, San (who could talk to animals), approached Ostrich. "Ostrich! Ostrich! I must

share with you the great dream I had last night. Oh King of all Birds, I saw you fly!" he exclaimed.

"I don't believe you. Why are you so cruel? You know I can't fly." Upset, Ostrich turned away. And with her back to him asked, "But tell me how I did it."

"It was the greatest thing I have

ever seen. You were standing in the strong wind that comes right before Sun rises. Your wings were stretched open and your eyes were closed. The wind came up and lifted you into the air. You flew like Eagle! You looked so beautiful," explained San with his eyes on Ostrich.

It sounded wonderful to Ostrich. She envied other birds for their ability. But no matter how hard she tried, she couldn't make her heavy body lift into the air. But now, what San said sounded so simple that she began to think it possible.

The next day, just before sunrise, just as the young San planned, Ostrich stood on the highest hill she could find. She stretched open her wings, closed her eyes and held her breath. The wind picked up. San, who was hiding nearby, crept right up to her and with one quick motion grabbed Fire and ran as fast as he could from there.

Realizing what happened, Ostrich was distraught. She wept and wept at the loss of Fire and the fact that she would never, ever fly. She was so upset and disappointed she became quite silly and forgetful. To this day, Ostrich remains one of the most simple-minded birds in the African bush.

As for the San, well, he continues to use Fire to cook his food, keep warm, and provide light at night.

And as is the tradition of the San, he shares it with others and never, ever abuses it.

THE FACT IS...

 It's believed that San are southern Africa's indigenous people. Their yellowish-brown skin, slanted eyes, and small size make them very different from the Bantu (or "Blacks") who migrated from Central Africa thousands of years later.

San live in complete balance with nature. They take only what they need and are careful not to abuse the plants, water, animals, or land. As part of this way of life, San often experience times of feast and times of near famine.

San respect nature and all it provides them. After killing an animal, all San say "I am sorry," and "thank you." Sorry to the animal for taking its life, and thank you to the animal for giving the San their life.

When water pans dry up or animal life is scarce, San find the water and food they need in over 80 species of desert plants. The tsama melon (Citrullus ianatus) is one of these water-filled plants.

San are well-known hunters, but they don't use guns. Their weapons include spears, and bows and arrows tipped with poisons made from different plants, insects, and reptiles.

Ostrich eggs first provide San with a meal, and when empty act as an excellent container for collecting and storing precious water.

Ostriches are the largest birds in the world. One ostrich egg weighs about 3.3 pounds. Cracked open, its insides equal nearly two dozen chicken eggs. That's some fried egg!

Ostriches are too heavy to fly, but they can run up to 40 mph. Their legs are so powerful they can break the jaw of an attacking lion with one kick.

TRY THIS:

RECREATE A DREAM (Art)

San pretended he had a vivid dream, which he then described. Can students draw a dream they once had? Distribute large sheets of drawing paper and crayons or markers. Ask children to draw a large bubble shape around the perimeter of the paper, which will be a frame. Then ask youngsters to draw a scene from an exciting or scary dream they once had. Invite volunteers to share their work with others.

PAPER AIRPLANE CONTESTS (Science)

Groups of children can participate in a contest to see which paper airplane flies the highest (or the farthest). To each group, give several sheets of paper. Ask youngsters to fold the sheets until they have one they want to enter into the contest. At the signal Go!, let each group's representative send their plane into the air. Which won? Why? Then ask children to make a new plane, based on the results of the first contest. How did youngsters modify their designs? Which won this time? Discuss.

HOW THE STORK CAME TO BE

Many years ago there were no Storks. In fact, there wasn't even a bird that resembled the Stork. At this time though, there happened to be a very insensitive man who lived in a large city in Morocco. This man was so cruel and uncaring that he used to invite people to his home only to play mean jokes on them, not because he liked them.

One day, dressed in his long white robe, which nearly touched the ground, and a large black hood draped over his shoulders, the man prepared for his guests. Although his invitation promised a huge feast, no table was set, no drinks were chilled, and no food was cooked. You see, the man never expected any-one to make it up the long staircase leading to his home. This insensitive man had smeared each step with a slippery clear grease.

As the sun set, guests began arriv-ing dressed in their finest clothes and

TRIBE
Unknown
COUNTRY
Morocco

jewels. Standing at the top of the stairs, the man smiled and greeted each person by name, beckoning them to come up the stairs to his home. One by one, the guests attempted to climb the stairs, only to slip and fall. Gowns ripped, trousers were covered in grease, one old woman broke her antique necklace and all its painted beads scattered down the street. The man thought the scene was hysterical. He laughed so hard he cried. Furious, his guests turned and stormed away, cursing his name.

A Powerful One, who knew of this inconsiderate man, saw the goings-on and decided something must be done. It only seemed fitting that someone with such an ugly personality be turned into something ugly. So the man was turned into an ugly old Marabou Stork. Forever more he would move about in his white body, black wings, bare pink head with a bright red hump right behind his neck. And if his appearance weren't enough to teach him a lesson, he is forever more to scavenge for his food.

THE FACT IS...

Morocco is a large country with many different ecosystems. Parts of it are quite fertile, where fruits like bananas and dates grow wild and in abundance. The Atlas Mountains run through the country and in winter are often snow-covered. Parts of the Sahara desert stretch into Morocco.

 Morocco is a Muslim country. One of the practices is that women must cover up—often from head to toe with only their eyes showing—in public. Another is that five times a day a *muezzin* climbs to the top of their holy building—a mosque—and calls Muslims to prayer.

Henna is a reddish dye made from a plant. Many people use it (even in the US) to color their hair. In Morocco, the women use it not only on their hair, but also to dye their hands and feet. Intricately designed stencils are placed over the woman's hands and feet. The henna is applied with a special brush. When the dye dries (after a few hours as the woman remains still) a beautiful lace pattern is left—a kind of washable tattoo.

In some Muslim communities, hennaed hands are considered a sign of wealth—a woman with elaborately dyed hands is one who does not have to work.

The Berbers and Tuaregs also live in Morocco. The Berbers live in the Atlas and Rif Mountains and are well-known for their hand-woven rugs. Their rug designs often tell a family's history. Many women weave patterns for future husbands that describe the man's wealth and life.

The Tuaregs, or blue people, get their name from the deep blue cloth they wear to protect their heads and bodies from the sun and blowing sand. They are nomadic peoples who cross mountains and deserts on camels and horses. They move between Morocco, Algeria, Niger,

Mauritania, and northern Nigeria, pitching their tents for months at a time in valleys or in the middle of sandy deserts near a water source. They often trade their camel-hair carpets, jeweled swords, jewelry, and hand-crafted wooden boxes for supplies from passing travelers.

TRY THIS:

MAKE A MURAL (Art)

Invite children to learn about Morocco today. After reading books on this country, suggest that children share their knowledge by drawing a large class mural. Decide on a scene they will illustrate, such as an outdoor open market. Divide children into three groups, one for each aspect of the mural: nature, people, objects.

Talk with the class about possible items for each topic, and list these on the board. For example:

NATURE	PEOPLE	OBJECTS
birds flying	women	blankets on ground with foods or necklaces displayed
trees	children	plants

Tape a large piece of paper to the chalkboard and have groups take turns drawing on the mural. When the mural is complete, ask the class what they like about their work.

FIND OUT ABOUT DESERTS (Geography)

Ask a student to point out on a map of Africa the Atlas and Rif Mountains and the Sahara desert. Looking at the entire continent, what other deserts can children identify?

HIPPO KEEPS HIS PROMISE

Long, long ago, when Earth was still young, Hippopotamus roamed the East African plains eating every tender green morsel he could find. As day turned into night, and night into day, Hippo ate and ate, growing fat and round. As summer neared, Hippo also grew very sad, for Sun's intense rays were too much for his enormous body to take.

Each day, when Sun was at her highest, and Hippo felt the most tortured, he would walk slowly down to River's edge. Here he would take a long cool drink of

water that flowed off great Mt. Kenya. As he drank, he often looked longingly at the deep green river and the fish swimming quietly about. How he wished N'Gai, the Creator, had made him a creature of the rivers and lakes. Oh, if only he could spend the cruel hot days in the coolness of the water, rather than in the dry, intense heat of the open plains.

TRIBE
Masaai
COUNTRY
Tanzania
(also Kenya and
South Africa)

On one particularly scorching day, when Sun felt stronger than she had ever felt on his tough hide, Hippo raised his head in agony and called out, "N'Gai! Oh Great Creator of all, please take me from these hot plains, and make me a creature of the water. *Please*, let me live like your beautiful fish in the coolness of River and Lake. I cannot take this heat, I will surely die!"

N'Gai looked down on this sorrowful beast and thought about his request. After some time, N'Gai replied, "No, I will not let you leave the plains for water. Your appetite is so great you would eat all the fish. You must remain a creature of the land."

On hearing this Hippo became frantic. Tears streamed past his enormous mouth. "Great One, please let me live in the water. I promise I will never, ever, eat your beautiful fish. You must trust me!"

"But how can I trust a creature as greedy as yourself? How will I

know you have kept your word?" boomed N'Gai, his voice shaking the trees.

"You will see, Wonderful One, that when Sun is high and bright, I will live in water and when Sun sets each day I will leave the water and roam the land for grasses and reeds to eat. To show you that I have not eaten your fish, I will come out of the water every night so you can check."

N'Gai thought about this and decided to give Hippo a chance.

Hippo kept his word, and to this day lives happily in the water, playing, sleeping, and walking about. At sunset you can see him leave the water, in search of tender plants to fill his great belly.

THE FACT IS...

Thousands of years ago many Africans began a slow migration from northern East Africa to Southern Africa. As a result, a variety of information was shared and passed from tribe to tribe. It's likely this is how this story made its way to Southern Africa.

Hippos may look fat and slow but they are aren't. When threatened or separated from their young they become extremely dangerous. Hippos kill more humans than any other African animal.

Hippo, elephant, warthog, and walrus all have large teeth made of ivory.

Hippos really don't swim; they walk on the bottoms of rivers and lakes. They can stay under water for nearly seven minutes.

Incredibly agile, hippos are capable of walking up steep, rocky paths. They are known to walk miles each night in search of food, some covering nearly 20 miles a night.

TRY THIS:

HIPPO RESEARCH (Science)

Visit the library and look up books on hippos. Talk about why hippos live in water. What might happen to them if their water source dried up?

IVORY RESEARCH (Language Arts)

 Research ivory. Talk about why it's such a valuable commodity. Encourage students to discuss why elephant ivory is considered so much more valuable than other animal ivory. Have them consider the size of the elephant's tusks, and the general size, strength, and power of the elephant.

PLACE NAMES (Geography)

Look at a map to locate the Ivory Coast. Do research to discover how it got its name. Invite students to present findings in an oral report.

STORY STARTS (Language Arts)

Write a group story explaining why different animals are the way they are. Here are some possible story subjects: How did lion get his mane, waterbuck his white ring, and rhino his baggy coat? Also read *Giraffe's Long Neck* and *How Leopard Got His Spots*.

PLACE THE TALE (Geography)

Locate Kenya, Tanzania, and South Africa on a map. Talk about the different geographic regions. Have students locate the equator and identify the countries it passes through. What do they notice about the Rift Valley— where does it start and end?

NOMVULA

"C ome, my zingane (children), gather around the fire," called the old woman from her reed mat. "I have a story to tell and I want you to listen carefully. It is a story about a young girl named Nomvula (you may know this name to mean rain), who failed to follow the words of her mother. Shh, now, wozani nizolalela (come and listen).

"Deep in the Ndumo forest—which as you know is not far from here— lived a beautiful young girl named Nomvula and her mother. Here, amongst the weaver birds, the shy nyala and quick red duiker, in the shade of an ancient marula tree, Nomvula had shared many, many happy times with her mother. But

TRIBE
Zulu
COUNTRY
South Africa

now, everything was to change. Her mother said it was time to leave this home and move to the village.

Nomvula couldn't bear the thought of leaving. It was here— under the marula tree—where she learned to weave and make beautiful beaded designs. And over there— just to the left of their hut—stood her garden and the bright green stalks of her mealies and the large prickly leaves of her pumpkins and beans.

Oh! How could she leave all this? Didn't her mother realize how many happy memories this home held for her? The more she thought about leaving, the sadder Nomvula became

72

until her mother thought something was wrong with her. And so the young girl begged and begged her mother to let her stay alone in the hut. She promised to do whatever her mother said, as long as she could stay.

Many days passed before Nomvula's mother made her decision. And then one evening, around the fire, Nomvula's mother sat her down and gazed into her eyes. "Nomvula, my beautiful child, I have thought hard on this matter," she said. "You may stay. But you must obey one golden rule: open the door to no one but me. You will know it is me by my voice, which you have heard since you were a child."

Deep in this forest, which seemed so peaceful and safe, lived a very clever beast who would be more than happy to make a meal of someone as young—and tender—as Nomvula. Nomvula promised to obey her mother."

"Would you like to hear more of the story?" the old woman asked the children. The children nodded their heads in unison, begging their grandmother with their eyes to finish. "All right, I will continue. . ."

"Now, each day Nomvula's mother would visit, bringing her a steaming pot of vegetables, maybe a little cooked pumpkin, and always some *putu* (say: poo-too). Nomvula looked forward to these visits, for in spite of the fact that she was quite happy with her memories in the tiny home, she missed her mother more than anything else.

One day, as Nomvula sat weaving a large colorful basket from the branches of the *lala palm*, she heard her mother's beautiful voice come floating through the forest.

> *Nomvula, Nomvula, Nomvula*
> *Ngqongqo* (Knock knock)
> *Vula umnyango ngingene* (Open the door for me to come in)

It was her mother! "Sawubona!" (Hello! I see you!) yelled Nomvula as she swung open the door. On this day, like every other day, the pair hugged and kissed before sitting down to share their meal. They ate and talked and laughed until the sun began to paint the sky a brilliant red. Now it was time for Nomvula's mother to return home. As she placed her colorful enamel bowl on top of her head, she reminded Nomvula to lock the hut's wooden door and open it to no one but her."

"As you know, dear children, in this forest lived an awful beast," said the grandmother, as she picked up a clay pot and took a sip of water.

"Well, one day, this beast was out

gathering wild herbs and onions for a stew. As he combed the forest he heard the most beautiful voice singing a very strange song.

Nomvula, Nomvula, Nomvula
Ngqongqo (Knock knock)
Vula umnyango ngingene (Open the door for me to come in)

Silently, he followed the voice through the forest until he saw a women with a large enamel bowl on her head. She was singing and walking toward a small mud hut that stood all alone in the forest. The closer she came to the hut, the louder she sang until the door swung open and a young girl ran out to greet her.

The beast scratched his head with his long dirty claws. He rubbed his eyes with his stringy tail. Could this be? A young child living alone in the forest? The beast began to drool and smack his fat lips happily. Resting on his haunches behind a fever tree, he watched the pair until the woman left. Only then did he return to his cave. The next day he retraced his steps and waited for the woman to arrive. Again, she sang her beautiful song, and the child opened the door."

"Now listen carefully, children. This beast was very clever and soon figured out a way to catch Nomvula".

"He tried to disguise his voice to sound like Nomvula's mother and approached the hut singing loudly and clearly. Nomvula heard the song but hesitated before opening the door. Something wasn't quite right. Shaking her head, she listened again to the song. 'Hmm, I think mother must be sick. Her voice sounds a little gruff,' thought Nomvula as she pulled open the door.

Well! Imagine the look on her face when she laid eyes upon the hairy, gnarled beast. Before she could scream or even think about slamming the door, she was stuffed into the beast's moldy sack and flung over his enormous shoulder.

'Oh! How could I be so silly! I paid no attention to the horrible voice. Now I will be eaten for sure.' With this sudden realization, Nomvula began to weep and weep. She wept so much it began to rain."

"Dear, dear children," said the grandmother who was wise beyond her years. "How could Nomvula do such a thing? Remember her mother told her not to open the door for anyone but her." The old woman looked at the children sitting around her. They were silent. "Well, it just so happens that this young girl was lucky. Very lucky".

"As the beast headed towards his cave with the sobbing Nomvula on his back, and the rain drenching his

74

filthy fur, he passed two hunters stalking a herd of impala. They heard Nomvula's cries and decided to help.

It didn't take long for these experienced trackers to find the beast and his sobbing sack. With one quick motion, the hunters sent their spears straight through the beast's heart. Nomvula was saved! The hunters released her from the sack and led her to the village and home of her mother.

From that day on, Nomvula listened carefully to what her mother said, obeying her every word."

THE FACT IS...

Author's Note: Margaret Ngubane, a Zulu woman, told this story. Her grandmother and mother told it to her and her brothers and sisters many, many times. She comes from KwaZulu Natal, a region of South Africa's east coast. This story, like many others, says Margaret, was told to teach her and her siblings to obey their parents. This is my version of her story.

In the early 1600s, a child named Zulu was born. He was the youngest of two sons and the favorite of his mother. Zulu's older brother, Qwabe, was jealous of Zulu and decided to kill him. Luckily, Zulu's mother learned of the plot and persuaded her son and a group of others to leave their clan. Together they created the Zulu tribe. It wasn't until six generations later that a new chief, Shaka Zulu, was named. It was under this chief that the Zulus became the most powerful, and feared, tribe in Africa.

Zulus believe their ancestors' spirits, or *amadlozi*, control their daily lives. Only the *sangoma*, or diviner, can communicate with the spirits. The amadlozi either speak to the sangoma in their dreams or through the patterns made when they throw the bones (a collection of small animal bones, shells, and seeds).

Zulus are great believers in the powers of *muti* (traditional medicines). To this day, everything from seeds to leaves and ground bones are used to heal the sick or troubled. The *inyanga*, or herbalist, is the one who creates the prescription.

 The Ndumo forest borders on Mozambique. It is home to hundreds of species of birds and a variety of animals, including the nyala and rare red duiker antelopes.

The Marula tree has a small oblong orange-colored fruit that is a little bigger than an olive. Each fruit has nearly four times the vitamin C as an orange and its pit is a source of protein. Elephants and other animals (including people) will walk miles for a taste of this fruit.

Zulus are well-known for their colorful beadwork, pottery, and tightly woven watertight baskets. Before white traders arrived in Africa bringing glass beads, Zulus made their own beads from seeds that they dyed different colors.

TRY THIS:

LEARN ZULU WORDS (Language Arts)

Write the following Zulu words on the board, and say them together. Encourage children to repeat them and then use them in their own stories.

zulu = heaven or sky
kwazulu = place of the people of the heavens
sawubona = I see you (standard greeting for one person)
sanibona = I see you (standard greeting for meeting a group)
kraal = traditional enclosure surrounding the village living quarters
inkhosi = tribal chief
induna = the headman
nkulunkulu = the Creator
putu = maize-meal porridge (maize = corn) (say: poo-too)

WHAT'S THE MORAL? (Language Arts)

As a class, discuss the moral of this story: Children should listen to their parents. Together, make a list of other reasons why children should listen to their parents. Can they think of any times when they shouldn't listen to their parents?

ZULU BEADWORK (Arts & Crafts)

 Zulus are famous for creating beautiful and unusual patterns in their beadwork and basketry. Have students draw and color their own designs, giving each pattern a meaning. Finally, have them explain the meanings of their patterns to partners or the class.

COMPARE-A-TALE (Language Arts)

Does this story remind students' of one they've heard before? Discuss how it's similar to or different from European fairy tales.

NOTES

NOTES